Title Withdrawn

W9-AEP-117

Dedicated once, twice, thrice:
To my son, Paul Doyen, who recited "Jabberwocky" with me.
To my mentor, Ann Whitford Paul, who insisted on a protagonist.
To my husband, Michael Doyen, who first showed me a Barry Moser print.
—D.D.

And for my friend Jeannie Braham.
—B.M.

Once Upon a Twice

By DENISE DOYEN

Illustrated by BARRY MOSER

RANDOM HOUSE NEW YORK

ONCE UPON A TWICE,
In the middle of the nice,
The moon was on the rice
And the Mice were scoutaprowl. . . .

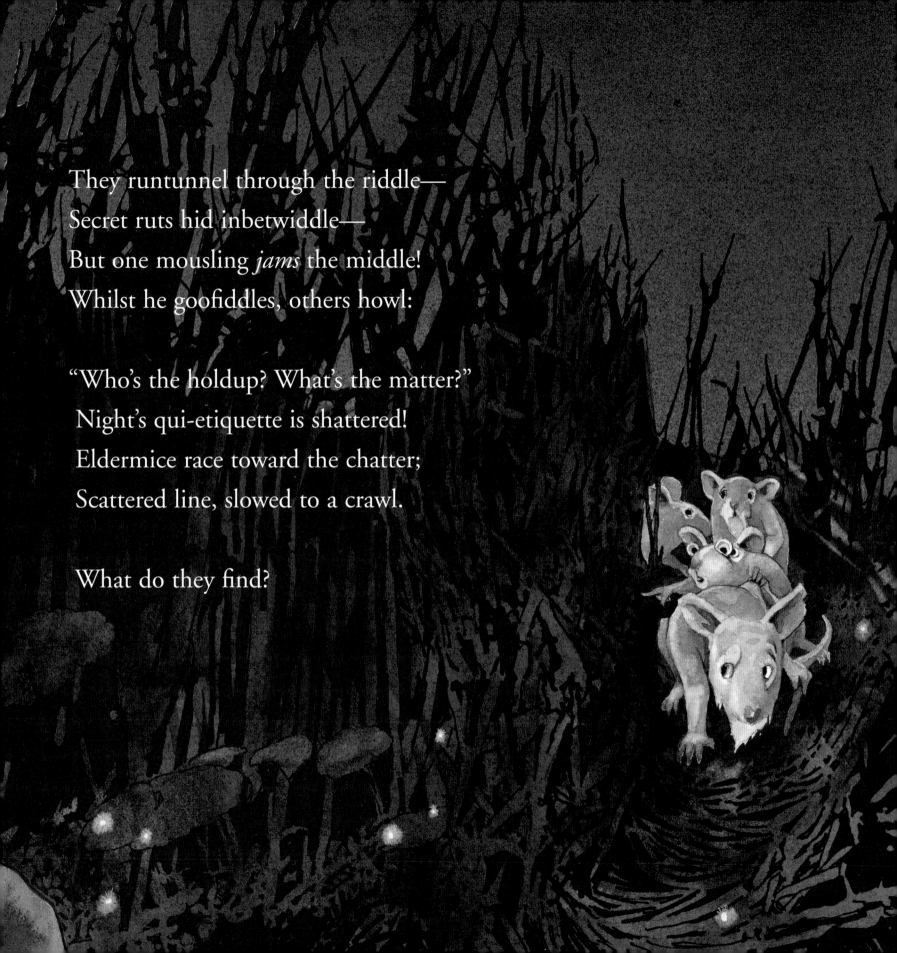

They runtunnel through the riddle—
Secret ruts hid inbetwiddle—
But one mousling *jams* the middle!
Whilst he goofiddles, others howl:

"Who's the holdup? What's the matter?"
Night's qui-etiquette is shattered!
Eldermice race toward the chatter;
Scattered line, slowed to a crawl.

What do they find?

A riskarascal in repose,

A mouse who stopped—to smell a rose.

"You there! Jam Boy!"—now he knows

His name, bestowed in front of all.

"You brought our scamper to a drag!
Dropped preycautions, raised a flag!"
Jam shrugs, he laughs, mouse-scallywag,
Brags, "I'm not a-scared of anything."

Aghast, the eldermice surround!

Jammed in the middle, he is bound

To hear their lecture: cold, profound.

A hounding Warning Song.

They sing:

"Beware the dangershine of Moon,
Do not disturb the bugs of June!"
The elder mouncelors whispercroon
A tune that tells Jam what to fear:

"Danger's lurking in the lettuce,
'Tween the celery, stalkers get us!
Open moonlight is a menace.
Trust in shadows—disappear.

"Cold eyes of gold watch without wink
For our ears and tails of pink.
From out the air, the field, the brink,
They slink up on a mouse at play.

"If those who swoop or them that pounce
Glimpse just a whisk! an inch! an ounce!
Jaw-claws will trounce a wayward mouse.
Renounce jamfoolery!
Go home and stay."

The knot of mice comes quick undone;
The rest resume their furtive run.
Jam starts for home, but then, for fun . . .

Shuns every warning, jumps the fence!

Jamagination in a flurry:
"I won't scamper! I won't scurry!
A clever mousling need not worry."
Furry overconfidence.

Off on his own, our hero, Jam,

Seeks adventure—on the lam,

Sneaks un -aware, -afraid, -asham'd;

He rambles past the haven reeds.

Jam Boy's breaking all the rules,
Enamored by a beetle's jewels.
Glassy water, shining dewels
Will fuel bravado, mouse misdeeds.

Out in the open, in the clear,
Where any wisenmouse would fear,
Jam licks his paw, he grooms an ear,
And never hears approaching *hisssss.*

Half-submerged, a slender queen
Esses 'cross the pond unseen,
Espies the furlickt mouse's sheen,
Sly serpentine—bound not to miss. . . .

There's a roil!—a coil!—a lash!

Ssssssssnake attacks! Mousling dashes!

Startled squeak-*eek!* A final *splash!*

Alas.

Silence descends like mud a-deep.

All the creatures round the beach
Hold their breath, their tails, their screech;
A silly mouse too brave to teach
Has reached his early dead a-sleep.

But no!

Jam scritchscrambles in a log!

Heart a-poundin', mind a-fog,

Disturbs a tadpole-tailed frog,

Then hogs her hiding place till dawn.

Skulking back—he hugs the walls,

Familiar, worn, grasshadowed halls

That lead to Sweet Home after all!

Rejoicing calls: "Our Jam's not gone!"

Mouse years go by. . . .

Jam, wiser whiskers now grown long,
Survivor, Keeper-of-the-Song,
Retells his tale of youthful wrong
To mousling throngs—a thrilling ham:

"When the Moon is full awake,
She's the ally of the snake.
You wanderyonder by the lake?
Make no mistake . . . you're in a jam!"

The world afield is dangerouse.
Foraging is—for a mouse—
A nightly knightly duel and joust.
The House of Mice has many mourned.

Remember:
Once upon a twice,
In the middle of the nice,
The moon was on the rice—
Jam's mice-advice is: "Be forewarned!"